The Courage Tunnel

Written By Joy Husted
Illustrated by Grace McKibbin

A Rhyming Story to Inspire 3 to 8-year-olds feel more Courageous

Published by Once Upon a Rhyme in 2021

@onceuponarhymebooks on Facebook

hustedjoy@gmail.com

© Joy Husted, 2021

All rights reserved

Set in Dyslexie Font Pt 16 : B504-4637-69DA-984A-CF7A-081E-6709

ISBN : 979-8-8486-5306-9

D1316368

ONCE**UP**❀**NAR**HYME

If you know just where to look,
there's something fun to be found.
Tunnels are in many places,
often hidden in the ground.

Tunnels can be manmade,
like a pipe or playpark slide.
They're also found in nature,
mostly homes where creatures hide.

One such little creature
who made tunnels for his home
was a fluffy little bunny,
who was not yet fully grown.

His name was Bobby Bunny;
his fur was grey and white.
The tuft of fur between his ears
was really quite a sight.

Most little bunnies love the dark
and even small tight spaces.
But the dark made Bobby oh, so scared;
he pulled the strangest faces.

He spent his days above the ground,
hopping briskly to and fro.
But when someone mentioned tunnels,
he didn't want to go.

Bobby's mama always told him,
"I know that you can do it!"
She knew that he was brave enough,
if only *he* just knew it.

At night when all the bunnies
snuggled in their burrows for a rest,
poor little Bobby slept out front;
it really wasn't the best.

Until one day it was so cold
that Bobby started to shiver.
A nasty breeze was blowing off
the cold and icy river.

His mom again encouraged him,
"Please come inside the burrow."
But Bobby simply shook his head,
"I'll maybe try tomorrow."

"To be brave," his mom explained,
"you can still be very scared.
It simply means that you have tried,
even though you feared."

"Challenges can be difficult
and courage is often needed,
but if you're brave and face your fears,
you'll be thrilled when you've
                              succeeded."

Bobby felt encouraged;
his fear was not so bad.
So he tried just one step further in
and started to feel glad.

"Well done!" cheered his mother,
and gave him a big cuddle.
The two of them then went to sleep,
all cosy in a huddle.

The next day Bobby had more courage
and took a few steps more.
He still felt scared but also knew
he was braver than before.

His mom kept on supporting him
and said she was so proud.
Bobby smiled and giggled
till it drew a little crowd.

The other bunnies welcomed him
with an excited greeting,
"Come through this little tunnel
where the others are all meeting."

So Bobby kept on going
even though he was quite fearful.
And when he reached the end,
the sight was happy and so cheerful.

The little bunnies cheered
with a big and loud, "Hooray!"
'cause Bobby's fear of tunnels
had finally gone away.

Bobby stopped and paused awhile
to ponder what he'd learned.
He realized that the title 'Brave'
was something he had earned.

He'd faced his toughest challenge,
one small step at a time.
Although he'd felt a little scared,
it had turned out rather fine.

From that day on Bobby ran
through the tunnel every day.
His fear was all forgotten
as he hurried through to play.

So when you see a tunnel,
whether natural or manmade,
remember Bobby Bunny,
and the bravery he displayed.

You can still be brave and strong,
even though you're small.
A tunnel can remind you
that there's courage in us all.

Being Brave

In a world that is constantly changing and where expectations are always shifting, children are faced with many challenges. Some of these challenges will seem harder than others and will require children to have courage to face them. When it comes to being brave, we sometimes just need a place to start or a reminder that we can be courageous. The Courage Tunnel was written to give children a simple yet gentle reminder that they can face challenges one step at a time. Bravery is not about feeling brave, but rather about facing your challenges even though you may be afraid. It is wonderful to be able to nurture bravery in young children. When doing so, it is helpful to consider the following:

1. Remind your child that bravery does not feel brave. You can explain to your child that being brave doesn't mean that you feel confident and capable; it simply means that even though you feel scared, you face your challenges anyway.

2. Narrate your own experiences of when you needed to be brave. Children often only see adults as being successful, confident and fearless. For example, you might say, "I felt so nervous on the first day of my new job, but even though I felt scared I went to work. I tried my best and it turned out to be a great day."

3. Openly embrace failure. Often a big obstacle to conquering a challenge is the fear of failure. If you can show your child that failure is a good and vital part of the learning process, they will be more likely to face their challenges with courage.

4. Positively affirm your child. Telling your child that you believe in them and praising their good qualities can give them the confidence they need to face their challenges. Even when they show the smallest amount of bravery by trying something new, you can encourage them to be proud of their brave actions.

Facts about Rabbits

1. Wild rabbits are very social animals and usually live in large groups called a fluffle or a colony.

2. Like cats, rabbits purr when they are happy and content. However, cats purr using their throat while rabbits make the sound by lightly rubbing their teeth together.

3. Rabbits' teeth never stop growing, but rather get worn down as they graze on foods.

4. Rabbits have eyes on the sides of their heads, which enables them to see all around them as they keep watch for predators.

5. Rabbits use their large back feet/paws to hop and jump up to 35" (90cm) high. They can jump up to 177" (450cm) horizontally.

Problem Solving and Reflective Questions

1. Can you find an earthworm on each double spread?

2. How many bunnies are on pages 16 and 17?

3. From the picture on pages 20 and 21, what do you think the bunnies are going to have for supper?

4. Identify the different tunnels on pages 22 and 23.

5. When you achieved something you were scared to do, how did it make you feel?

Once Upon a Rhyme series

Stories to encourage social and emotional development:

Once Upon an Antelope - Anger management
Once Upon a Crocodile - Learning to embrace differences
Once Upon a Giraffe - Managing stress and anxiety
Once Upon a Hippo - Dealing with loneliness
Once Upon a Hyena - Choosing kindness
Once Upon a Bush School - Celebrating strengths
Once Upon a Recipe - Story for fussy eaters

The Good Reminder Series

Join Lerato the Tortoise as she encounters a Kindness Door and is inspired to start her very own kindness project.

Join Jeremy the Hedgehog in this delightful story as he discovers the trick to having a grateful mindset.

Join Bobby the Bunny as he conquers his fear and learns that even though he is small and feels scared, he can also be brave.

Find out more about these books on Facebook @onceuponarhymebooks

These titles can be purchased in the USA from www.amazon.com as paperbacks or on Kindle (some titles are available on Kindle Unlimited)

Made in the USA
Coppell, TX
13 September 2022

83029959R00017